Crow loudly and lay daily.

Tasha V. Meisenheimer

PIA PULLET

COMES TO CHICKEN LITTLE FARM

TASHA V. MEISENHEIMER

Dedication

To my son, Lachlan James, whose unwavering curiosity made me a storyteller.

To Maegan who first sparked my passion for poultry and entertained every whim of mine.

Copyrights

Copyright © 12th July, 2022. Tasha Marie Meisenheimer

All rights reserved. No part of this book may be reproduced or used in any manner without written permission of the copyright owner.

ISBN: 978-1-959532-40-8

First published in United States of America in 2022

Registration Number TXu 2-327-838

Effective Date of Registration: July 12, 2022

Registration Decision Date: August 01, 2022

Copyright Registration for One Work by One Author Registration issued pursuant to 37 CFR 5202.3

Title Title of Work: Pia Pullet Comes to Chicken Little Farm Completion

Publication Year of Completion: 2022

Author: Tasha Marie Meisenheimer

Author Created: Short Story

Citizen of: United States Domiciled in; United States

Copyright Claimant: Tasha Marie Meisenheimer

953 Grassy Hill Rd, Orange, CT, 06477-1101

Certification Name: Tasha Meisenheimer, Author/Owner

Dated July 12, 2022

It was a pleasant, sunny day on Chicken Little Farm. All of the Red Cross chickens were busy playing in the yard. Chelsea, Charli, Chandler, Charity, and Choyce played their favorite game while Regal Rooster and Chesney stood at the side and watched them play.

"Oh! You cannot beat me in this game because I am the best!" exclaimed Chelsea, the biggest chicken. Chelsea was very conceited and rude to the other pullets because she thought she was the prettiest one.

"I would have won the game if you didn't get in my way. Why do you always ruin things for me, Chandler?" Charli complained. Charli, a fat and stumpy hen, was very clumsy. She always fell, slipped, and placed last in most games. She constantly blamed others for her shortcomings.

Chandler was angry that Charli blamed her and retorted, "Oh, don't blame me, Charli! You always lose because you are clumsy and don't know how to play at all!" Chesney and Regal were interrupted by the bickering chickens and came to intervene.

"Stop it, both of you. Why are you always fighting?" Chesney asked. As she approached the flock, she tiptoed around the mud and dirt. She prided herself on being clean and tidy. She was very shiny and didn't like to take dirt baths like the others.

Charity giggled as Chandler and Charli argued. Charity cared more about visiting the cute cockerels near the side fence. She often daydreamed and enjoyed drawing hearts in the dirt with her little claw.

Even though Choyce was out in the yard, her attention was consumed by the upcoming Town Fair. She stared at a poster tacked up on the barn door that showed a picture of herself with a blue ribbon on her chest. She had hopes of winning again this year.

Regal had been living on the farm for a very long time. No one knew exactly how old he was and no one ever asked. When Regal spoke, everyone listened, even if they didn't like what he had to say. Most of the pullets did not like having to go into the coop at night. They wanted to stay out late and play. They also didn't like eating their daily ration of oyster shells, but Regal insisted that the calcium was necessary for them to lay healthy eggs.

"Come on now, pullets. Don't start fighting over the smallest things. We are all friends here, aren't we? Friends don't fight when they are playing together," instructed Regal. The chickens returned to the game, but as soon as they were about to start, Mr. Little, the farm owner, came into the yard holding a beautiful Polish pullet. The Polish pullet had an enormous plume of feathers on her head. Only her bright orange beak protruded, looking like a small carrot.

He released the Polish chicken among the hens and smiled. Immediately, Chelsea and Choyce became envious, seeing the look of adoration in Mr. Little's eyes. They thought she looked ridiculous.

"Hello ladies, this is your new friend Pia; say hello to her," announced Mr. Little with a wink and a tip of his hat.

All the Red Cross chickens formed a group and gazed at Pia in amazement and surprise. Chelsea clucked and Choyce squawked. They had never seen a chicken like Pia. They observed the color of her feathers and scrutinized the summit of feathers on her head. In turn, they looked at each other's heads. None of them had such a thing.

"Hey, what is that thingamajig on her head?" Charity whispered to Chelsea.

"I don't know. Something's wrong with her head. I can't even see her eyes," Chelsea snickered.

"She doesn't look like us at all. Is she even a chicken?" Choyce asked.

"She is strange," Chandler said, a little disgusted.

Charli watched as Mr. Little headed back to the farmhouse. Then she inspected Pia and said, "She's really skinny, too."

Pia became frightened and turned her head from side to side. Pia was very timid and felt anxious because the chickens glared and circled her saying hurtful things. Chelsea came close to Pia and sniffed her. "She's different than us. Let's not play with her." Chelsea headed back to the coop, and all the hens followed her except Chesney, who lingered. "Come on, Chesney," hollered Chelsea.

Chesney looked at the coop, then back at Pia. "I think your plume is a beautiful tiara," whispered Chesney. Pia smiled for a moment at the kindness Chesney offered.

Chelsea came running back to Chesney. "Why are you here?" Pia explained that Mr. Little had seen her at the tractor store and decided he wanted to bring her to his farm. The other hens came trickling back to Pia.

"What is wrong with your feathers? Where is your crown, like we have?" Choyce asked as she shook her red comb and wattle.

"Nothing is wrong with my head and feathers. It is just how they are," Pia answered.

"Maybe she is not a chicken. We are chicken, and this is what we look like. She does not look like us at all," Charli concluded.

"Maybe her crown is under her feathers," Choyce suggested. All the chickens gathered around Pia.

"Yes, maybe Choyce is right; let's see what is underneath those silly feathers," Chelsea said. All the chickens gathered around Pia and pecked at her head and body.

"Ouch! No stop! I am a chicken. Ouch, please stop!" All at once, Pia's feathers floated to the ground as all six pullets aggressively plucked her head. Pia pleaded, "I am a different chicken. I don't have a crown like you all have. Please stop!"

Regal heard the commotion and came running to the rescue. "Stop it! All of you stop, you little juveniles! You are hurting her! I am ashamed of every single one of you!" he shouted. Regal's racket immediately stopped the pullets from attacking Pia, who was crouched in the dirt, disheveled from the assault.

"Move away from her. Is this how you welcome a new friend?" Regal scolded the chickens. "Apologize right now! All of you," Regal ordered, shaking his head. While Pia stared down at the ground, she saw her feathers form a perfect circle. They shimmered in the dirt. Half-heartedly, they apologized, but as they walked away, they gave her dirty looks. Pia picked up her discarded feathers, and Chesney helped her.

The next day the chickens came into the yard after they had eaten lunch. The sun shone brightly. The pullets started playing "Chicken." In this game, each chicken had to run toward another one. Whichever hen stepped aside first would lose. Chesney convinced Pia to play, and she reluctantly stepped up across from Charli. Both hens charged toward each other, and Charli side stepped first. "Yah! Pia, you won!" celebrated Chesney. Charli was furious. She squinted and said she lost because the sun blinded her. Pia stood there with her eyes shaded by her feathers but said nothing.

A few days later, the sky grew dark with thick clouds, and a rumbling could be heard. The rain came pouring down. All of the Red Cross chickens scattered, dashing to bushes along the fence for shelter.

"Move out of the way! I don't want to get wet and sick," Choyce said as she used her girth to push the other pullets out of the bush.

" I look sad and ugly when I am wet," moaned Chelsea.

"I hate being dirty!" cried Chesney as she preened her feathers from under the bush.

Pia, however, didn't run at all. She was confused that the hens were hiding in the bushes. Her large plume saved her from the heavy rain. The rain splattered in the dirt, helping Pia to find worms easily. A chipmunk came up to her for shelter, and she offered him to come under her feathered umbrella. Together they shared a tasty meal. The chipmunk helped Pia find even more worms.

The Red Cross chickens watched from the bushes, and Charli was jealous that Pia was eating all of the plump worms while she ate nothing. The irritable and hungry hens were jealous. They had lived on the farm longer than Pia, but they had never befriended chipmunks. The only friends Chesney and Charity had made were the young cockerels on the other side of the fence. Chesney was impressed by Pia's plume of feathers, but the rest of the Red Cross chickens were still not convinced.

The following day Mr. Little came out to the coop. He opened the door, and the hens came racing out. He scattered seed and left to head into town. All of a sudden, they heard a loud screeching from the sky.

"Kee-aahh!"

They looked up and spotted a huge, hungry hawk flying over their heads. Immediately scared, they ran to and fro, trying to outmaneuver the hawk's sharp talons as it swooped down to grab them. Regal saw the hawk and ran out, squawking as loud as he could. Pia was too far away to get to the coop safely, so she stood completely still in the tall grass. Using her head feathers, she was able to blend into the grass and not be detected. The hawk circled above, looking for a chicken to snatch. Chelsea and Chandler ran into each other and fell over before they could safely get into the coop. The hawk then flew away, never having seen Pia. Chelsea looked at Pia and then at the terrified chickens and reassured, "Regal will always be here to protect us from the hawk."

Several days later, Pia noticed all of the Red Cross chickens were cleaning themselves and preening their feathers. She quietly asked Chesney what was going on. Choyce interrupted and said they were preparing for the Town Fair. Choyce pointed her claw to the faded blue ribbon hanging outside the coop.

"I won first place last year," she said proudly. "And I plan on winning again this year, too." A moment later, Mrs. Little entered the coop wearing a pretty white cotton dress and a large sun hat. Instantly, she reached for Pia. All of the hens stared at Mrs. Little as she carried Pia to the pickup truck. "Oh no," Choyce cried. "She didn't pick me this year. She didn't even look at any of us!"

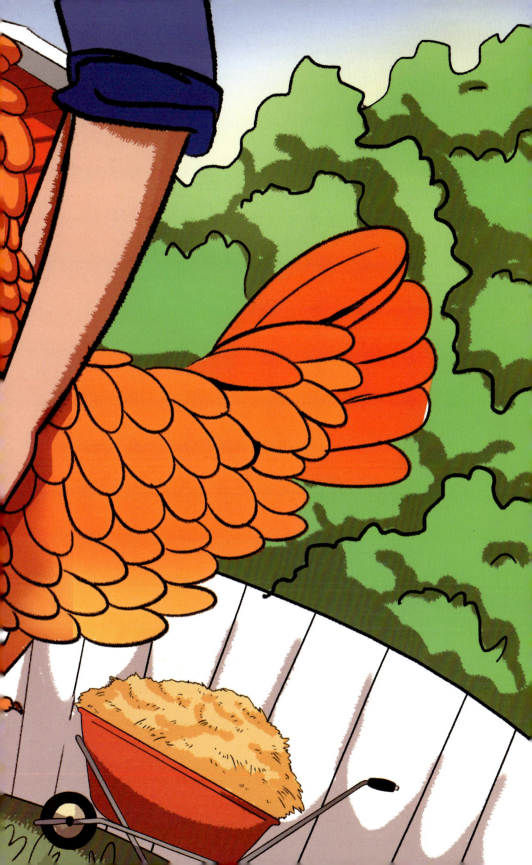

Charli said, "And I spent all this time preening my feathers for nothing." The Red Cross chickens were dejected and sad that none of them were going to the Town Fair. Choyce ran to a nesting box and sobbed uncontrollably. Chesney and Charli tried to console her while Chelsea paced back and forth, enraged. Regal sat on the white picket fence, watching everything unfold. He shook his head in disappointment.

Early evening the chickens heard the Little's pickup truck pulling into the farm. They all sulked. Mr. Little removed Choyce's faded blue ribbon and tucked it in his pocket. He then hung up a new bright blue ribbon. "Good evening, ladies. Look what Pia won today." He was so pleased with Pia and smiled.

As he walked away, Choyce's faded ribbon fell from his back pocket and blew away down the gravel path. Once again, Choyce burst into tears and buried her head under the straw. Pia saw how distressed Choyce was and how sad all of the other chickens were.

"I thought I was the most beautiful chicken, but I am not," said Choyce in a muffled voice.

"Yes, I guess we are not as pretty as Pia; we will never win a blue ribbon again," Chelsea said glumly.

Charity interjected, "We don't have that glorious plumage on our heads. How could we ever compete?"

"No, no," said Pia, "You are all beautiful without it. You have beautiful, fluffy red feathers and big yellow eyes that sparkle. You have vibrant red combs that match your wattles perfectly. You shouldn't want to change a thing."

Seeing how depressed and downtrodden the hens were made Pia sad, too. Suddenly, Pia had an idea. She lifted her nest and found all of her feathers that the hens had plucked from her head the very first day she arrived at Chicken Little Farm. Pia joined the feathers in a perfect circle to make an elaborate, fancy headpiece.

She then brought it over to Choyce and gently placed it on her head. All of the hens' eyes bulged with excitement. "Oh my, Pia. It's so beautiful. I look like a queen, don't I?" exclaimed Choyce as she strutted in front of the medal feeder, admiring her distorted reflection. Pia nodded in agreement. She then busily made a second and third headpiece with her feathers and placed them on the remaining two hens.

They batted their eyelashes and agreed that they would wear their headpieces when visiting the cockerels. Chesney helped Pia weave the final three headpieces for the remaining hens. Chesney proudly put hers on and looked at Pia. "Now I have a tiara too!" Chandler reluctantly bowed her head for Pia and joined Chesney.

Chelsea was overwhelmed by all of the excitement but still seemed to harbor resentment toward Pia. Pia approached her and said, "These silly feathers do block my vision quite a bit, so be careful the next time there is a hawk in the sky." Overcome with remorse, Chelsea apologized to Pia with sincerity. Pia flipped her head feathers back to wink at Chelsea. All bad feelings were forgotten.

Throughout the next year, the pullets used their feathered headpieces while playing yard games. Since her eyes were shaded from the sun, Charli managed to win a few rounds of "Chicken" against Pia.

One fall afternoon Charity lingered a little too long at the fence clucking with the cockerels. When she ventured back to the coop, she spotted a fox peeking into the window. She hid in the tall grass using her headpiece to blend in, standing perfectly still. The fox crept away.

And Chandler made a few new friends with the squirrels and groundhog when she offered her head umbrella in the rain. She never knew the groundhog was such a funny critter!

When it came time to prepare for the Town Fair, Choyce and Chesney were excited to get everyone ready. Chesney fluffed each feathered tiara, and Choyce placed one gently on each chicken's head.

Later that evening the chickens settled in their nesting boxes to go to sleep. They all looked up and clucked when they saw seven blue ribbons hanging on the coop door. Regal caught a glimpse of a faded blue ribbon blowing down the gravel path. He turned to the hens and said, "When we celebrate what makes us different, we become united. When we share a small part of who we are, we uplift everyone. Even if it is as light as a feather."

The End